About the Author

Hello, gentle readers, I'm Annie! I don't have any degrees, I dropped out of college twice, and I don't have many concrete skills, but I can occasionally mildly entertain people in casual conversation and I guess I tricked myself into believing that was enough to write a book.

The Untold Stories of Mr. Snuggles

Annie Kartalia

The Untold Stories of Mr. Snuggles

Olympia Publishers
London

www.olympiapublishers.com
OLYMPIA PAPERBACK EDITION

A CIP catalogue record for this title is
available from the British Library.

ISBN: 978-1-80439-596-7

First Published in 2023

Olympia Publishers
Tallis House
2 Tallis Street
London
EC4Y 0AB

Printed in Great Britain

Acknowledgements

Thank you to my Padre Goose #papaG for being the first and loudest supporter of my writing

Prologue

And there he lay, sprawled out on the teal, crushed velvet, wingback upholstery which he had claimed as his own by deeply embedding his fierce talons within the fifty-fifty artificial and natural fluffing. Although his intentional and fairly destructive representation of dominance had cost me my beautiful, once sage green, $20 chair from Goodwill, it warmed my heart to see him making our new space his home. Before we get ahead of ourselves, let me introduce myself.

Hello, gentle readers, my name is Annie. Some might say I am an unapologetically hilarious nineteen-year-old innovator stuck in a warehouse job where my only creative outlet is finding the most efficient way to stack boxes. While I do realize my current career path is essentially a never-ending game of Jenga, it has its benefits. Like the super fun guessing game of, "Will my coworkers psychologically harass me today?", as well as the several paid holidays I had to give up after my new meds and anorexia decided last week that eating was a back burner problem which quickly led to me desperately trying to dig myself out of this unfavorable and wildly unpromising hole I had created.

That being said, I feel like I've slowly been inching toward this project, and I think the time has finally come.

Ladies and gentlemen, gays and theys, it is with a humble heart that I introduce to you what could possibly and most likely be the greatest recorded story of all time; *The Untold Stories of Mr. Snuggles*, a historical fiction novel written by me, Annie;

biggest stan/proud mother of this beauticious and let's be real, the most important creature to ever exist.

So, grab a snack, hit a blunt, and join me on this wild ride of potentially made-up or historically accurate (Imma keep the mystery and leave that to your imagination) tales of a tail and most importantly, the beast attached to it, :)

Chapter One

Shmoodle's Christmas Story

Last Christmas morning with my baby bear was probably the highlight of my life. This little man exhibited multiple signs of angelic behavior. "Angelic behavior" in the sense of life-saving properties, as well as his otherworldly presence. Did this man also develop violent tunnel vision and attempt to snatch the treats Santa delivered, even if it meant striking me to do so? Absolutely. But for anyone who knows Mr. Snuggles, that's pretty standard behavior. Before you call me a bad mother, let me teach you some Shmoodle history.

When I first met Mr. Snuggles at the shelter, he was, how shall I put, big chillin'. Round as a rustic farmhouse boule bread, he lay, which seemed to me like an obvious sign he was trying to communicate an unspoken, satirical narrative about America's "cookie cutter" pet. As a whispered chuckle slipped through my parting lips, I had the most eye-opening realization. This cat was my son. Biological or not, this small gentleman was meant to be in my life. The way he defiantly rejected the historically degrading idea that any animal other than man is rightly subject to ownership amazed me. For so long, I had been told, and we as a people have tricked ourselves into believing, homo sapiens are the world's smartest animal. I am here to debunk that myth. Everyone always assumes Mr. Snuggles defies basic orders like, "Cover your shit," or "Don't eat all the goldfish snacks," because he's dumb. He's not, he just chooses to be an asshole. This then sets us up for the rest of the story…

Okay, so, it's the night of Christmas Eve and I'm at home with my most beloved baby bear. He's loafing on the carpet again. And while that sounds like a gentler way of describing a release of excess bodily fluids, loafing is actually a deliciously precious sleeping position wildly popular among the feline community. As I reach for my phone to capture the beauty before my eyes, he lets out an excited rumble and breaks into a light jog (some could say a rushed jyalk[1]) into my open arms. The soft sounds of "A Putumayo World Christmas" fill our quaint home as I hold him softly under the warm glow of the high-strung lights. At this point, I'm nearing a joyful tear.

The clock strikes twelve. It's Christmas morning. I plant a much-needed kiss on my baby's soft forehead. It's time for treats and Shmoodle is more than ready to feast upon the catnip-flavored "Temptations" treats stuffed within the custom stocking, handmade with love by my roommate.

Immediately following the reveal of the nibbles, Mr. Snuggles's pupils dilate in a ferocious manner, a look I've seen countless times. This man is out for blood. The best way I can describe this sudden change of heart is the same way a werewolf turns under the light of the full moon. In the presence of food, Mr. Snuggles is no longer filled with any amount of love. He is filled with a vicious obsession; an obsession I partially blame myself for. I think about how it could have been me, his crazy mother, who passed down this unfavorable trait. Not to say that I love him any less in these moments, because that is a false statement, and I say that with full confidence, but it aches my heart to see him struggle in an instant without the comfort of food.

But it's Christmas and he deserves it.

I place a few treats in the palm of my hand and lower them to a reachable level for the little man. A tame yet unpleasant bite following an excessive amount of violent sniffing is just what I expected. But I'm not mad about it. That's just Mr. Snuggles for you. My boy is crazy, but I love him.

After devouring a good handful of treats, I put them up on a high shelf and let him settle down. Once the food craze subsides, we curl up together on our cheap, royal blue, velvet couch from Amazon, which surprisingly turned out to be much cozier than the stiff, board-like sensation we were expecting from the stock photo. We flip on our TV and play our favorite cartoon, *Adventure Time*. Life is good.

Also, fun fact: Mr. Snuggles ended up breaking into the hard plastic treat container off the shelf, eating it all, and barfing it up on my rug later that morning.

Footnotes

1. Jyalk
   /yÔk/
   verb
   A relaxed jog/walk whilst talking with your friends.

Shmoodle Watching: An Advertisement

If you're struggling with a lack of feelings such as happiness, love, excitement, and bliss, Shmoodle watching could very well be for you. Much like bird watching, this relaxing yet thrilling experience requires little effort on either's part. You, the watcher, have one simple task; gaze upon the small gentleman as he amazes the world with his living and breathing properties. You're gonna say, "That's a crazy cool creature you just introduced me to!" or a full money-back guarantee.

Tips and tricks for beginners:

- Consider dabbling in the devil's arugula beforehand.
- Angles, angles, angles. Get on his level and witness the beauty from the perspective of the beast.
- Lure the tiger into a sunny patch and wait for a few moments to calm and collect yourself and do not look directly at him as the sun hits to avoid blinding your eyes from exposure to pure majestic energy. If you're willing to endanger yourself for the chance to see a miracle, this guide may not be for you. You may need to upgrade to a master's guide for full entry to tango with the gods, aka chill with the lovely yet daring Mr. Snuggles in the glorious light of our lively star.
- Bring a camera to record your reactions to seeing the man in his full flesh form.
- Turn on an avian documentary of your choosing and catch the beast in wilderness mode.

- Play music to heighten feelings that may arise.
- The man has got hops, so be sure to put those rumors of agility and speed to the test! Use a laser pointer for speed, and a feather wand for leaps and jumps!
- Never feed Shmoodle and attempt to pet him at the same time. It is possible but takes a great deal of training and skill and is only available to master guide users.
- Keep hands and limbs out of his bubble for safety reasons. If you are to approach the beast, and I ask you to do this with great delicacy, present your hand and let him come to you. And DON'T get too confident. Less is better.

Music Recommendations (you can play these when you meet him):

Beautiful Boy (Darling Boy) – John Lennon
Jaws Main Theme (From *Jaws*) – John Williams
this is what falling in love feels like – JVKE

Pricing and Plans:

One hour visit - $400 per person
Five minute visit - $50 per person

Mr. Snuggles will be accepting a maximum of five lucky winners for a personal meet and greet! You must still pay the price for whichever plan you end up picking, but don't you forget that you could be one of five people in the entire world to get the incredible opportunity to pay $50-$400 to see my cat in person for up to an hour!

I think you're ready, kid, now go make your dreams come true.

Chapter Two

The Miracle Before the Slumber

I just witnessed something incredible. So elegant he lay, so mysterious he appeared. I took a photo. I can't show it due to intoxicating levels of ethereal and sumptuous energy, but i can try my best to describe it for you. Not only am I deeply moved and soul-touched right now, but I'm also kind of freaked out on all fronts. First, what if I had been asleep at that moment? I was literally about to snooze for a real one before that happened right before my eyes. It's times like this when I turn to God and thank him for his extreme clutchness, although these conveniently awesome occurrences are usually short-lived due to grave, perilous situations he decides to humble me with. But let's not dwell on the negativity. Let's talk about this picture.

It's intriguing, it's innovative, it's the work of an artist. His existence is a masterpiece in itself, but to go the extra step and create a form so crazily majestic is truly inspiring.

He's long yet stout, a deadly combo. Hiding his money maker in the down comforter, he perfects the illusion of mystery. I say illusion because Mr. Snuggles wears his emotions on his sleeve. He's an open book, really. Some people think it's rude when he viciously attacks them, but I think it's beautiful how he accepts his feelings and can showcase them in an honest and transparent way. He teaches me something every day. Maybe that's why I'm such a conniving bitch.

And if you thought the picture was crazy enough, Imma blow your mind right now with this next piece of information.

So, I went to dip my toe into the pool of possibilities, poke the bear if you will. I grazed his “M” stamped forehead with my newly-tatted knuckle. At first, nothing happened. I laid back down and was about to attempt a lengthy slumber when all of a sudden, I hear a faint, high-pitched rumble. I moved my head closer to the sound. You guessed it. It was Shmoodle. He was snoring. His lumpy-like figure rose and fell with each breath. And every few seconds the small wheeze would reappear and warm my heart. And on that happy note, I did in fact indulge in a comatose-like shut-eye.

Warm love: A Poem

When I look at you, my heart feels warm
Like a cozy fire with a big sweater on
You’re my home, you’re all I need
With you around, my life’s complete

Chapter Three

A Chill Night in With Shmoodle

Most nights are chill when Shmoodle is present. You can always count on him to be his sedentary, lump-like self. He is so unapologetically him and I think it's safe to say we can all learn a little something from the man himself, Mr. Snuggles, aka the fearsome beast, aka my precious baby boy, aka the main character in, not only this story, but every story till the end of time because when it comes down to it, not even God himself or any otherworldly presence could face this small gentleman and live to see another day and if you don't find that totally epic, that's your first mistake. And is that a slight exaggeration? No, absolutely not. This entry might as well be published in a renowned scientific journal because the work we do here is not only completely factual in every way but legendary to the max. Are you picking up what I'm putting down, comrade?

Sorry, got a little carried away, but it's so hard not to when he's perfect in every way <3

While Mr. Snuggles is entirely capable of mass destruction and international obliteration, most of the time he's not in the mood. This dude knows how to lounge. In fact, L.L.Bean personally reached out on numerous occasions, pleading and begging for reconsideration of their valuable offer to be the face of the company. It was a whole ordeal, but basically, Shmoodle was like "Nah," and now we live in a two-bedroom apartment with a roommate we met online. Which is fine, but we could have been living in a two-bedroom apartment with a roommate with also lots more money in the bank. But Mr. Snuggles is a man of the people.

The crazy thing about this whole situation is that a very similar situation occurred, but instead of a cozy clothing line asking for partnership, it was The Devil himself asking for him to be a hell spokesperson. And that speaks volumes about him, and I could not be prouder of his multifaceted personality. But again, same issue. It all came back to his humble roots.

He said and I quote, "It is far less satisfying to be rich in riches than rich in humility."

And I was like, "Woah, dawg, that's profound."

Although he said it with his eyes, the message was more than clear.

Let's get back on track, folks. It's time to describe in frustratingly great detail what it is like to experience a chill night in with the man of the hour, Mr. Snuggles.

The clock reads six-thirty p.m. The time is now. I grab a tall glass, who are we kidding, it's a plastic cup, fill it with cool but not too aggressively cold tap water from the horrifically messy kitchen, and take it back to my room where I display it on my side table. I say, "display", partially because I like the sound of this particular verb and also because, if I'm being totally transparent with you, it usually ends up becoming a useless prop in the background. It's not because I'm anti-hydration, but more because I just never get thirsty, and I cannot elaborate on the history of that fact because I am not entirely sure myself.

After I pretend to take care of my physical well-being, I like to make my bed so Mr. Snuggles has an aesthetic place to rest his paws, obviously. I then turn down the stress and turn up the bass in my speakers as I play an aquatic sounds playlist on Spotify. The LED lights are set to blue, and you best believe that the aquarium light is on.

I would like us all to take a moment of silence for our brave soldier, Sandra the beta fish. May you live a blessed afterlife and let us wish all the suffering that led you to jump out of your tank where you were then devoured by Mr. Snuggles has come to an end. So little time we had together, so strong an impact you had on our lives. Rest in peace.

Shmoodle sits in an italicized loaf. His round head bowed, his eyes closed but not clenched, ears up but not perked. I let out a small gasp of disbelief, I mean, valid because I just witnessed something beyond compare, and Mr. Snuggles leaps up, like the agile little man I always knew he could be, and courageously gallops into my hands where I squish his face and scratch his head.

Precious.

I'm sparking up and it would be impolite to blaze without offering an invitation to join. I unscrew the small jam jar of catnip and place a small pinch upon the navy throw on which he stands. A few gentle sniffs quickly escalate to a more extensive olfactory investigation. The boy is hooked. We have officially entered zooted territory. I know what to do next.

I flip on the avian documentary, *Dancing Birds* on Netflix and let Shmoodle gaze upon the quick and colorful creatures. You can just look at him and tell that his cranial sponge is doing some real intense work. Gears are turning, lobes are heating up.

All is still for a moment. The world has gone silent. We await the tiger's response. Whatever happens is up to him now, the future in his paw. Will he lunge at the screen? Run away at lightning speed all the way from my room to the front door and then casually make his way back? Or will he turn that chaotic energy on an unsuspecting third party who will remain nameless solely for superstitious reasons but who is also the only other creature in the apartment seeing as my roommate has fled to Mexico briefly?

I guess we will never know because I never finished that thought, but I am taking full credit for that being a super intentional cliffhanger.

Mr. Snuggles: A Poem

Sweet and doughy like a barred owl
Fierce and regal like a great horned
The way he slinks is like a weasel
The way he shines like a star
He's the winner and the prize
And sure, could bring you to your demise
But he's kind at heart, a noble lad
He's one-of-a-kind and pretty rad

Chapter Four

Meow! Smack Attack

Once upon a time, Mr. Snuggles was playing with a feather wand. It was precious and an undoubtedly baller presentation of his star quality, so I snapped that shit! Of course, I had to post it to the gram. Click, Clack, he's on the map. Praise came pouring in, reviews rolled in (all positive, obviously). None of the comments seemed to faze the man in the slightest, he has a very much Selma mindset.

For those who aren't familiar with Selma, it's a small, bite-sized book of contentment about a sheep who had the opportunity of living her eternal dream and chose her current life. Selma didn't do much, just ate, played, and chilled with her fam (paraphrased), and it's the same for Mr. Snuggles. He sleeps, he lounges, he decompresses and sunbathes. A little scamper, a sprint or a strike gets the sillies out for the night. That's the reason I love him or one of the many. Just existing is a job well done. Every breath is a miracle, every sight a blessing. He lives in the moment, and while most of the time, I'm debilitated by the fears of the future and past, when I slow down to his level and take that much-needed pause, I too am in the moment.

So, when UFC hit my boy up for some in-person action shots of last week's smackdown, he was less than impressed.

Shmoodle's a simple man, and all the hype he was receiving seemed a little too much. But what you may not know about Mr.

snuggles is that he's a Capricorn. And while the human Capricorn doesn't quite fit the bill, I found a page on the internet that gave me the feline star sign inside scoop, and, yes, I will be taking all this info to heart. According to pawp.com, Mr. Snuggles' star sign is the reason for him taking this job. He's a working man and appreciates a task every now and then. Oh, right, I hadn't gotten there yet. So, he took the job. Thought we could use a little cash, cash going toward his many treats, of course.

Next thing you know, we're at the arena. Shmoodle stepped one paw in and immediately regretted his decision to blow the mind of every young American interested in televised fighting. His tummy rumbled in a rugged rage. I barely remember the night; it was like a fever dream. The way the lights shined down on his jet-back feathers was almost too majestic I blacked out. Thankfully I regained consciousness just in time for the drama.

A man followed by a herd of cameras approached him. You could see him heating up after having had his bubble popped by a loud, ugly, bald man. I could tell this was about to be quite a performance.

"Meow! Smack Attack legend, Mr. Snuggles, Snuggs for short I'm assuming." The reporter threw his eyes toward the small gentleman's general vicinity like a sheep without a shepherd; lost, confused, and looking for guidance. Mr. Snuggles, ferociously annoyed by the ramblings of an uninformed idiot loser, puffed his silky front feathers and did what he does best. Like a sugar glider, he spread his flaps and smacked down with a most vicious fury. The crowd went wild, applause roared. With a humble glance and a heavy huff, he slunk off the stage and took off on the most sensational journey, retirement.

Chapter Five

The Ferocious Mutilation of Mr. Mouse

Twice upon a time, Mr. Snuggles caught a mouse. His first catch of the year was by far the most horrific thing I've ever witnessed. So there I was, chilling in the hot tub, totally unaware of the bloodbath to come. Mr. Snuggles was just outside the tub, exploring like the adventurous little kid he always has been. I heard him scurrying around, so I popped my head out of the tub to gaze upon his fluffy face. Little did I know, his face would have a little mousy edition dangling from his fangs. At first, I was so excited for him. He doesn't have much practice as a hunter because of his domestic indoor cat nature, so his rodent catch was quite impressive.

He looked around in an apprehensive stance, seeming not quite sure what to do with his latest conquest. After several moments of uncertainty, he gently placed his victim on the cement patio. As soon as his fur touched the ground, the little mouse made a run for his freedom. Mr. Snuggles quickly placed his paw firmly on his head, leaving him immobilized and scared. Shmoodle's eyes kept wandering as if searching for guidance on whether or not to commit an act of violence on this harmless and delicious-looking snack. You could see his conscious and inner demon tussling for control over the situation. Seeing him in turmoil was heartbreaking, but I knew this was a decision he had to make for himself.

He lifted up his paw just for the mouse to make a break for it once again. This time, Mr. Snuggles pinched the mouse between his canines and stood motionless for about five minutes. The suspense was almost too much, but right when I thought I couldn't take it anymore, Mr. Snuggles refocused and chose violence.

He chomped down in a bestial rage. You could hear the snapping of bones and a small wheeze from the creature he carried. Shmoodle dropped the wounded soldier on the unyielding surface and ripped his skin straight off. I felt shivers through my body as I watched this live-action nature documentary. After picking apart and digesting the small mouse, he stepped back and reflected on his choice. A wave of mixed emotions washed over him, leaving him with an empty and shameful look on his face. I jumped out of the jacuzzi, scooped him up, and planted sweet smooches on his head, hoping all this love would diminish any sore feelings he had.

"It's okay, Shmoodle," I reassured him. "It's just nature."

Day In The Life: A Poem

Like a rotisserie chicken, he lay, like a saber-toothed tiger he slay
With white tux and mittens, he sat prim and fittin'
Like a wild kitten villain who'd slain a beast from the dwelling
Even the demon inside needs a little cuddle at times
After a tiring and hardworking day
So I scooped up the muffin and gave him some lovin'
Three pecks then he's off on his way
To eat up a creature or watch a double feature

Of his favorite film then snooze the day away
Once he’s up from his nap, I give him a pat
And start it all over again

Chapter Six

Reminiscing on The Little Ladies

Mr. Snuggles and I moved out. The lease was up on our apartment, so we moved back in with the parental units. So far, it has been good. Aside from freedom, our biggest loss was the kittens. They didn't die, but we will never see them again. Sad thoughts call for reminiscing on the little ladies. So please enjoy this memory I resurrected from my dome piece.

A tussle. A tumble. All that's heard is a small rumble. From whom? Was it birdie, the delicate desert fox? Or her circular-shaped sister, Miss Chickadee? The lumpy lady in question hobbles around the corner and dives her flat head into the carpet as she rolls onto her back, looking to the obvious father figure for love.

Shmoodle is taken aback. He forms a funky face as he readjusts his paw positioning, presenting as regal as possible in such confusing times. What is the root of this confusion? Let's backtrack. Chickadee is the feline daughter of our roommate. Lumpy, like a certain beige-colored starch, Miss Chickadee is as lovely as she is deluxe. But Miss Chickadee is a scared little lady, scared as a small flightless bird. But today, she was brave. She not only accepted the gentleman's love but sought it out. This could have been a beautiful moment if Mr. Snuggles had not responded by biting her face. But he did.

Miss Chickadee ran away. How could he have been so cruel

to nip her in the nose when she had shown nothing but courage and bravery? Dejected and blue, she slunk back into the depths of the sock drawer where she silently wept herself to sleep. Just a baby cat she was, small and round, now shedding a tear among the comforting coziness of fresh laundry. How heart-rending. I feel my eyes getting a little too refreshed as I narrate this tragedy. What can I say, I'm an empath.

But not to fret, gentle readers, Miss Chickadee's inaudible distress was brief due to Shmoodle's sudden change of heart. Like a sneaky mink, he slithered into the forbidden room of our roommate, on the prowl for his redemption arc. Mr. Snuggles stretched his long torso up by his mittens, sniffing the sock drawer intensely. The articles of clothing rustled and shifted as Miss Chickadee pushed her noggin to meet Shmoodle's.

Their noses sparked as they touched, sending them both running away from each other. They may be away now, but I know the love in their hearts will ring eternally <3

Chapter Seven

Daring Dance-off

Practicing my Britney Spears spins in the mirror, I caught a glimpse of Shmoodle's judgmental and elusive stare. His quick glances and attitude-filled face was throwing me off so immensely. I stopped spinning and darted my competitive eyes to my opponent.

"I challenge you to a dance-off," I foolishly jabbered.

How ridiculous of a statement as I type it now, but, in the moment, I was heated by my fanciful passion for poppin' and lockin', a passion that has gotten me in far too many sticky situations.

Maybe popping and locking isn't in his wheelhouse, I thought to myself, knowing damn well that this little man has the talent of a thousand circus performers. He was a star and I was just a silly girl with a jam in her heart and no real dancing ability. I had no chance at this competish and that was not only a severe bummer but also a gosh darn drag. A hefty huff of regret left my freshly balmed talking pillows.

But let's look on the bright side. I get to watch Mr. Snuggles perform a dance routine! This could be the most revolutionary day ever and I was about to witness it first-hand. I then felt like the luckiest person in the world! How silly I felt for having wasted my precious time feeling blue over a minor loss. I still chose to dance my heart out though; never waste an opportunity to shine like a star.

After warming up our glutes and such, we took to the stage.

Mr. Snuggles wore his blue bowtie, impeccable class. I wore a faux alligator skin tuxedo and a peacock feather in my hair too, ya know, keep it simple. Shmoodle sat prim and proper, his head slightly downturned, mysterious yet daring.

The music started.

Mr. Snuggles puffed his silky front feathers and shimmied across the floor. He let out a low rumble as he hoisted himself into the sky like a delicate bird and landed perfectly on all paws like a true champion. It was so beautiful that I almost shed a tear. He then flicked his paw in a deliciously scrumptious interpretation of modern dance. That was the final devastation. I might as well have packed my bags right there and then. So elegant of an ending to that beautiful journey of physical expression. I was speechless.

I hobbled up to the stage where Mr. Snuggles had so recently lit it up with his groovy moves. How could I possibly follow that? The answer is, I couldn't. Once I broke out my below-average robot, the crowd roared with such hate in their hearts. An old queen with a glass eye and a look of utter contempt threw a raw potato right at my gullet. Thankfully, this was all happening in my imagination, so no esophagus was beaten by starchy veggies. But the pain of self-discontent and loathing was still very much real.

To My Precious Darling Sweetheart: A Poem

What do you see in this boy they say
He's vicious and suspicious and evil to the core

I say yes but he's the best; each day I love him more
It's crazy because I mean it; it's sweet because it's true
To my precious darling sweetheart, my life is full because of you

Chapter Eight

Rainy Days

It's Sunday. The pitter-pattering of the midafternoon rainstorm sets the tone for the day. Mr. Snuggles is curled up on the rug under the window. He lets out a small wheeze as he stretches and adjusts his nap form. So fluffy a creature he is, so deliciously precious. His paw is tightly pressed into his velutinous button nose. I play lo-fi beats through my speaker as I munch on honey nut cheerios and journal. I devour some edibles from the local dispensary and sink into the comfort of my sage green wingback. After a while, Mr. Snuggles migrates over and nestles himself into the blanket that covers me.

Loud rumbles emanate from his body. He kneads his paws into my stomach. His talons are like razor blades. It hurts like a bitch, but I hold back the tears. Thankfully, the giggle bites I ate kicked in and the thoughts of pain and distress melted away like a raspberry sorbet on a hot summer day. I felt Shmoodle's happy vibrations hum through the upholstery and into my heart. We sat contently for a good two hours before the rain stopped and the clouds parted, revealing a beaming sky of sunshine. Mr. Snuggles leaped across the living room, seeming rather curious about the outdoors.

"What is it, Shmoodle?"

I ran to the window. I slid the glass door aside and stepped my pigs onto the cold, wet concrete. Yuck. But on the other hand, there was a rainbow! A big, beautiful, misty rainbow was just the thing we needed. I wiped off a chair and popped a squat. Mr. Snuggles stepped back into the carpeted floor and basked in the beautiful bright rays of a hopeful spring.

Chapter Nine

The Miscalculated Conundrum

He sat betwixt the leaves and sticks, stalking his prey by night. His gleaming greens pierced the dark sky and created an ominously beautiful contrast. Those big eyes made their way through the dense shrubbery path and over the hill. I followed close behind. Every so often, Mr. Snuggles would stop, sniff the air, and recalibrate his route. Route to where? We are not sure.

He seemed so focused, a vigilant beast. His tail swept from side to side in a ferocious and feral manner. His crisp, white whiskers stuck out like quills on a porcupine. He was onto something.

The nearly full moon sat on the countryside horizon, the air cool and eerie. It was the perfect night for a midnight prowl, and Mr. Snuggles was more than up for a late-night excursion. He sped up his trotting pace and shifted gears into a slinky sprint. His shiny fur glistened in the moonlight. His quick paws moved effortlessly through the tall grass, his tubby tummy trailing shortly behind. He was a vision.

Over the cinderblock wall and around the stone pizza oven he traveled, leading to a clearing just beyond the flower garden. He came to a halt and sat his soft tush on the dew-covered floor. He scanned the scene carefully and meticulously. Something was wrong. He let out a low yowl and stomped his pearly white paws in a vicious rage. After a few moments of reflection, Mr.

Snuggles turned and headed home. He spent the night curled up on the windowsill, gazing at the moon and chattering. He seemed to be waiting for something, but I couldn't figure out what.

The next day, at sundown, Mr. Snuggles set off again over the hill and past the garden. As he entered the clearing, I could see a shining, almost blinding light. It was the moon. No, not the moon. His eyes! His eyes glowed white beams which shot forceful fire into the ground where the light of the full moon shimmered. I felt my head pounding with pressure as the flames grew higher. I fell to the ground, my vision blurry. Everything went white.

I woke up in my bed. What a strange dream.

Chapter Ten

Toe Pluckin'

Pluck. Crunch. Bite. These are three verbs that could very well describe the actions of Mr. Snuggles' grooming technique. He sits slouched on his lower back, paw propping him up, toe in mouth. He pulls away quickly and scrunches his face tight like a lion before a kill. He darts his face back in with another swift bite and high-pitched growl. As I watched him gnaw on his heel, a tornado of thoughts clouded my mind. Thoughts like, this creature is UNREAL, as well as a burning desire to make ASMR videos of him. Talk about a moneymaker. So, I did. I grabbed my sonyrx100 camera and got to shooting. Lights, camera, action.

Mr. Snuggles flexed his paws and looked at the camera. He was a star. He spread his toes, his talons out. Pan left, zoom in. The vision was coming together. He licked his soft fur down, burying his face in his tummy and biting his roots every so often.

A few edits and splicing on iMovie and this footage will go down in history as the most deliciously enchanting and wildly captivating film. Or, at least, that's my guess.

I followed his movements with the camera, getting low to the ground to get his best angles. It was too easy; the camera loves him. I zoomed in on his face, capturing his every detail. The brown highlights of fur beautifully contoured his facial features. His nose sat snatched above his lip, dragging down from his rugged brow. He slow-blinked into the camera; I pointed it at his iris. His vibrant greens pierced the lens with their dazzling and exquisite beauty. If you looked closely, you could make out the yellow flecks of color sprouting from his pupils. Stunning.

He threw his foot in the air, pointing his beans to the night sky. The moon was bright and bold, much like Mr. Snuggles. It shined through the window and struck his velutinous snoot. He let out an itty-bitty sneeze and blessed the universe with a groundbreakingly adorable release of shnozz air. Shmoodle shook his head and licked his lips. They were most likely salty from sneeze residue. Ew. He turned to look at me. I guess he could tell I had been fangirling in the corner for some time.

"Hi, sweetheart," I rang to him.

His eyelids lay heavy, blanketed over his glossy eyes. He gave me another slow blink. I sent one back. Blushing, he turned away and got back to the task at hand. He dampened his paw and massaged his cranium. It was breathtaking. After cleaning the dome, he moved to his mittens. He plucked his toes in a rhythmic wave of ethereal -

"Annie, shut up!"

Bittersweet: A Poem

Sometimes I wonder if I talk about Mr. Snuggles too much.
The love that I feel sometimes feels too much.
If we ever departed my heart would die.
It sounds silly, but he's my whole life.
Believe it or not, he's my best friend.
He doesn't tell jokes; he just sits there and grins.
He lights up my life, my sweet baby boy.
That cat over there? He's my homeboy <3

Chapter Eleven

When the Cat's Away

Mr. Snuggles woke up with an adventure on his mind and a song in his heart. He was feeling antsy from all the lounging at the house and needed a little getaway. He waited by the back door all day until someone finally opened it, slipped through their feet, and slithered off on his journey. Through the corn fields, past the hedgerow, and over the hill he scurried, looking for a sense of purpose in this big world.

Shmoodle stopped at a pond and rested his paws. He lay close enough to the water to look in and admire his reflection. He carefully dipped his paw in. A fish swam to the surface to nibble at his toes. Mr. Snuggles threw a swift blow to his gut, got up, and set off on his trek through the countryside. The sun was setting, the clouds were beautiful shades of pink and orange. The colors grew more vibrant and all-consuming. The sky sat over the world like a painted dome of feminine rage; mother nature sure was feeling fiery. Just ahead, a wooden bridge appeared. A blossoming willow hung heavy above the bridge and the water running beneath it. Pink petals fell softy on the path. Mr. Snuggles' tail started shaking.

Who was this? Mr. Goose! A lumpy, white goose stood in the middle of the bridge. Mr. Snuggles approached him with ease and reached his head in for a good sniff. Mr. Goose did the same. A small spark later and they're back for more sniffs. Mr. Goose leaned his head back as he shook in excitement. His beautiful white feathers shimmered in the setting sunlight. Mr. Snuggles looked down at his feet nervously and back up to gaze upon the sun-kissed poultry. The energy was sweet and romantic.

Do you hear that? Someone nearby must have started playing smooth jazz because the tranquil harmony of sax and low fi beats showered the two lovers in a blissful ambiance. Mr. Snuggles bumped his head up under Mr. Goose's chin and nestled into his silky chest feathers. Mr. Goose wrapped Shmoodle in his long neck and held him warmly under the colorful sky and into the night. The stars glistened; the moon shined. It was heavenly.

For a moment, Mr. Snuggles felt his demonic rage die to a low purr, and a surge of serotonin burst through his lumpalicious figure. This was happiness.

As the sun rose over the fields, Mr. Snuggles knew his date was over. He sat up and looked Mr. Goose in the eyes. Tears puddled over his gorgeous greens as he turned away and headed off on his journey back home.

The heartbroken, dewy-eyed goose sat hopelessly as Mr. Snuggles disappeared into the distance.

Mr. Snuggles knew he wanted an adventure, but he never expected to fall in love.

Heartbreak: A Poem

Shmoodle sat on the basement windowsill
Looking out solemnly
His heart felt heavy, his spirits low
But could you blame him? He had lost his beau

A beau who sparked his love for geese
Not in a carnivorous way but a love in peace
He made him feel calm, safe, and secure
That’s a bond he’ll cherish for sure
But until he heals, he’ll feel all the feels
Cuz let’s be real, the boy was head over heals

Chapter Twelve

The Toasted Tussle

One day, I made some toast. No wait, it gets crazy. Trust me. So, there I was, standing innocently on the kitchen tiles, waiting for my toast to crisp in the white, metal toaster. My mismatched socks wriggled as I shifted my weight to my left foot. One sock had patterns of black and white while the other had an explosion of colors. The colorful foot stood planted on the cool, hard floor, low and exposed. Mr. Snuggles waltzed in. It had been a hard day, so seeing my little monster peek his head into the room made my heart sing.

"Shmoodle!" I rang as he came jogging toward me. How foolish I was to expect sweetness. After rubbing my legs, he dove his head into my foot and opened his trap of fangs. I quickly darted my foot back and stood horrified by the counter. It wasn't a full-on attack, but it was dangerously close and ferociously upsetting. The boy had laid a paw on me. It wasn't the first time, and probably won't be the last. We sat there in silence for several moments. He started licking his foot. My heart was breaking and Mr. Snuggles didn't even care. But that's how it goes, I guess. After his violent grooming sesh, he made a break for the exit. Running away from his problems, again.

The toaster popped.

"Don't think I won't write about this in the blog, Mr.," I declared as he rounded the corner where he then nested in the cat tree. I couldn't stay sad long, he was just too gosh darn cute.

And believe it or not, that was the whole story. I did say it was going to get crazy and personally, I think this story was intriguing as hell, but I might be a little biased. Never trust a stranger, especially when that stranger is a cat-obsessed loser. But thank you for reading :)

Sunday Morning: A Poem

Bright and early he's up in my bed
Biting my face and licking my head
He's ready for food and I'm ready for sleep
Even though I just finished hour thirteen
But he's loud and persistent so I get on my feet
And hobble to get his morning treats
I plop back to bed where I dream of more rest
One more hour until it's time to go

Second Wake Up: A Poem

Shmoodle loafs upon the throw
I turn to meet his face
He looked at me, eyes glazed
And yawned away the morning haze
We don't want to leave
The puffy hug of mattress fuzz
It surely was a dream
But the day calls and our ears are open
So we get up and get to hoping
For a good day and the ability to slay

Chapter Thirteen

Feeling In My Flop Era

Feeling like I'm in my flop era. I went to a party tonight; I left early. My loser love for feline friends has brought me back to the depths of anti-socialization once again. I find the more I hermit, the more I crave alone time. Alone with Mr. Snuggles, of course. He's for sure my favorite creature. Something about chatting all night with a lump of expressive fur just hits the spot. There's no pressure of filling the silence and no stress in "feeling on". I've been having this problem as of late and it's a severe lack of linguistic ability in conversation. I'm not sure if it's anxiety related, which could make sense because I stopped taking my anxiety meds after I decided the taste was too unfavorable, but it's been putting a real damper on my groove. When I'm chilling with the Mr., I don't have to worry about how I present or what percentage I'm operating at. It's nice. I wonder if this is something I should snap out of or lean into for the time being. I worry that I'll never want to be around people because, at this point, I'd be cool if I never had to go out again. Although knowing myself, this is probably a phase.

So, it's the end of August, and Mr. Snuggles and I are curled up on the bed, watching *Buffy the Vampire Slayer* in the newly decorated Halloween room. And it's the best. It's just what I want to be doing right now. And I think that's a good way of looking at things. Right now is not forever. At some point, I'll probably want to go out more, but staying in, writing, and chilling with Mr. Snuggles is the perfect thing for right now.

Chapter Fourteen

Scratch-and-Sniff Kitten

It's spooky season. I'm so excited. You could say I'm mf jazzed, for a few reasons. Halloween, the festivities, the costumes; they're all great. But what I'm most excited about is my scratch-and-sniff kitten. Mr. Snuggles' fur takes the smell of the outdoors, and fall is one of my favorite smells. Autumn musk plus his underlying smell of bread, Mr. Snuggles' coat in October is divine.

The jack-o-lantern is lit, the spider webs hung. Shmoodle sits on the top step of the front porch, looking regal as ever in his festive bandana. Scout, my parent's dog, wears a matching one. The two majestic creatures sit beside one another and wait patiently for their photo. How sweet. I snap a shot and tuck away my phone to free my hands for head scratches. I rush to them, hands open. They lean their heads in, graciously accepting the pets. I run inside to get their treats; a rawhide for Scout and a salmon squeeze for Mr. Snuggs. I tear open the Gogurt-looking salmon puree and let Shmoodle take a whiff. He takes a sniff, and immediately devourers it, licking violently like a ravening beast. Miss Scout sits politely, rawhide in both hands, gnawing her treat like the best little lady.

After their treats, I decide to take them on a walk. This is tricky. Finding a way to get the harness on Mr. Snuggles is like doing arithmetic while plummeting to your death, it's difficult.

Difficult but also incredibly scary. Somedays, it is not possible. But this day it is possible. I leash up my girl Scout and hit the road. Except it isn't the road. It is my backyard because Mr. Snuggles decides his journey ends at the end of the back patio. I unclip Miss Scout from her trail running attire and watch as she chases not only her dreams but a small bird. Her droopy ears fly to freedom as she gallops through the yard. Mr. Snuggles is eating a small bug under the picnic table. I crouch down and level with him. He breaks into a jog and gives me a noggin-to-noggin attack of friendship. It is appreciated, but boy, does that kid have a crunchy head. I scratch his face and chin; he melts into a puddle of fur and rolls onto his back. A gust of cool autumnal breeze whisks through his luscious locks. I scoop him up and bury my nose in his chilled coat. He smells like October. He smells like carving pumpkins on the porch. He smells like fall. It truly is a miracle.

Muffin in a Basket: A Poem

Muffin in a basket
He's so sweet
He sits upon the onions and beets
Why he goes there, we don't know
We just try not to cramp his flow
He'll sit there for hours at a time
Soaking up the aroma of loose basil and thyme
Delicious always, but now even more
Muffin in a basket, who wouldn't adore?

Chapter Fifteen

The Friendship Journey of Mr. Snuggles and Scout

Let me tell you a story. A story about a sweet pup and her fierce and sharp brother. So, Mr. Snuggles had been a staple in the fam for a good seven years. After his darling sister Mini passed, he had become an only child and the only "pet" in the house. And he got used to that lifestyle quite fast. On one frightful day, the parental units brought home a pup. She had a brown head and a white speckled body. She had a brown splotch across her back. Her eyes were bright blue. She was just about the size of Mr. Snuggles at the time. As she wobbled, her wrinkly skin swayed side to side. It was so precious; however, Shmoodle was not amused. I still remember his reaction, mainly because I took pictures. Immediately, when Scout (said pup) entered the house, Mr. Snuggles was distressed. He sensed her presence and was totally not jazzed.

As Scout rounded the corner to meet his gaze, Mr. Snuggles made the first attack. He struck her across the face, hissing to add to the injury. She was taken aback, for sure, but this little lady was not giving up just yet. She leaned her snout back in, hoping for a somewhat civil response. Unfortunately, Shmoodle was in no mood for camaraderie. A swift punch to the jaw and Mr. Snuggles was on his way to the basement for shelter. Scout ran after him and stuck her head through the cat door. This game of cat and mouse, who for some reason, likes pain, went on for about five years.

After those five years, Mr. Snuggles and I made the courageous decision to move into an apartment downtown. Scout was devastated. She had lost her only brother. She spent days looking down the cat door, wishing for a miracle. A miracle of his return. Little did she know, he was to return a year later. Life had taken some unwanted turns and we ended up back at the parents' house. Scout was overjoyed. But this time, she made sure to keep her cool. No longer would she dart her face into his face looking for a fight. She was grown now. And this grown lady was going to show Mr. Snuggles her new maturity.

Shmoodle stepped in the door and took a little walk around the house. Scout sat, eyes wide, by the couch.

As Mr. Snuggles strode past, she resisted the urge to agitate him. He was impressed. Never before had she been so calm and collected. Could this be the start of a friendship? I think yes. Scout's new restraint was quite the turning point in their relationship. Mr. Snuggles continues to warm up to the gentle canine. Yesterday, I caught him head-bumping Scout's chin; it was a beautiful moment. They may have had their ups and downs, but I believe their love will only grow stronger.

Slay: A Poem

Mr. Snuggles slays in a couple of ways
Let me break it down
He is a king, he wears the crown
He's got the fury, had a whole smackdown
Where he bit the lip of the whole establishment

He's a titan, he's a god
The boy is fully clawed
He can serve, he can swerve a paw into your jaw
The boy is kind and divine and hard to define
I think he's pretty slay and I think you'd say the same

Chapter Sixteen

A Worry-Filled Wednesday

Today was a lot. And tonight, I thought I lost my heart. I had let Mr. Snuggles outside while I went to grab something inside. When I got back to the patio where I had let him loose, he was nowhere to be seen. I ran around the house, calling his many names. Nothing. I was getting frightened. My chest felt tight. It didn't help that it was pitch black out. The only light was the crescent in the sky and the phone flashlight in my palm.

Where, oh where was my baby boy? Had he boinked down the groundhog hole like he had tried to do not so long ago? I hope not. Mr. Snuggles doesn't have "street smarts". Or I guess "country smarts" would be more fitting. He grew up a city girl, not a country mouse, so it's hard to blame him for his lack of marmot knowledge.

When we got Shmoodle from the shelter, we had to sign papers promising we wouldn't let him outside. And for some reason, we also had a home inspection. Weird, right? But we did what we had to do to take him with us. He was just too special to let go of. So tonight, when I called for him and got no response, I panicked. Running around like a chicken without a head, I looked like a fool. I missed my son, my little ghoul. I would do anything to see his face. And all of a sudden, I did. He came trotting over and meowed at my feet. My heart exploded with love and happiness. How long had it been? Three minutes? It felt like an eternity. I swept him off his feet and cradled him like a basket. I hustled him to the door and let him inside. What a relief. I felt the pressure in my chest dissipate. I felt all my worries melt away. Everything was going to be okay.

Secret Feasting: A Poem

As I munch on my cookies, I hear someone crunching
I bet I can guess who it is
He's light on his feet, a sneaky attack
Must be the cat with Cheezit crumbs on his back
He's soft, sand-silky except for the debris of the cheese
That sticks in his coat like a lock with a key
I sit him outside and wait for the breeze
To swoop down and clean his fur with ease
Once he's free of the cheese, I give him a squeeze
And wait for his next feasting needs

Chapter Seventeen

If You Give Mr. Snuggles a Salmon Squeeze

If you give Mr. Snuggles a salmon squeeze, a lot could happen. Your heart could burst with joy overload, you could lose a finger in the crossfire. Hand placement is key to maintaining safety. Once the boy has got a taste of the meat puree, he goes into a feral carnivorous frenzy.

Snap, crackle, pop; the seal was broken and the aroma of creamed fish wafted its way into the beast's nasal passage. These savory fumes struck a vicious chord in his being. He wrapped his paws around the Gogurt-looking tube and grasped it tightly. His lips snarled as he consumed the nutrients with a savage passion. He was here to feast. And feast he did.

I sat on the carpet while he sat on the chair. I held the base of the treat package steady as he devoured the goods. He was so precious. I snapped a video, of course.

As the squeeze tube got thinner and thinner, he grew more ravenous. He started looking elsewhere for food, aka my flesh. He licked my hand up and down and when that wasn't enough, he went to take a bite. Luckily, I was on the lookout for this behavior and was able to sneak my hand away just in time. I waited for his emotions to settle before reaching my hand to his face.

I scratched his chin and gave his head a little pat. He leaned into me and snuck in a quick love bite. So sweet. I threw out the remains of the treat and headed to bed.

If you ever get the chance to give Mr. Snuggles a salmon squeeze, take it. At least, for me, it was an intensely emotional journey of love and light. He really does make the world shine brighter.

Window sitting: A Poem

Sitting at the window
Cackling at birds
He's so delicious, it's hard to put into words
But I'll try my best, and first, I'll address
His whimsical chatter caused my heart to shatter with joy
But nevertheless, I too did persist
Fangirled too hard and crumbled I'll admit
But I'm back on my feet, watching him clatter his teeth
At the colorful creatures who once were reptiles
With his background beat, I began to freestyle
Bars on bars about Shmoodle watching crows
There are lots to see while sitting at the window

Chapter Eighteen

Flash in The Future

I'm trying to picture my life in the future. And this seems to be all I see. Call it intuition or premonition but I think this is how it'll be. We're living in Pittsburgh, in a small, character-filled townhouse. There's a bay window, obviously. The floors are hardwood. There's life right out the window; there's a symphony down the street. Mr. Snuggles sits on our balcony, plucking at his feet. The weather is mild, it's partly cloudy. And most days, it's pretty foggy. But we like it here, we dig the vibe. It's fun and peaceful and one of a kind.

Our days are spent living, both wild and mild, chill yet fulfilled. It's nice going out, but I like our place much more. We have a backyard with a fence and a goose on the loose. Her name is Noodle, she's soft and white. When Mr. Snuggles saw her, it gave him quite a fright. But he warmed up quick, after a peck and a lick, and then they were best of buds. A cat and a goose? The critics were weary, but the love is real in our animal sanctuary.

I got another cat, or I should say, Shmoodle did. He grabbed her by the face and gave her a sniff. Next thing you know, they're bundled up like two cats in a bundle. Their cuteness fuels my heart. The kind of cuteness that inspires my art, art of the pen doodles or art of words. These two rascals will be a hoot and a half for sure. I can't wait to meet you, and neither can Shmoodle. Whatever your name is, I'm sure you will also love Noodle!

I hope I'm still writing, still spitting out rhymes. Sometimes it's the only thing that makes me feel alive. Something about linguistic gold has really got me joyous. Keeping the creative flow is surely the best thing for us. We write. We craft. We share a laugh. It's wholesome and sweet in our house of many treats. I feed each of the cats a small piece of jerky. They rip it apart like two sturdy perky turkeys feasting on berries.

On weekdays, I work part-time, something simple and doable. But nights are always spent with the kids and their chicken chewables. Shmoodle and the kitten can be found tussling under the table. They tussle until they are no longer able. After their exercise, they gaze at the setting sky from the comfort of the window. The two lovely lumps fall asleep under the stars and the moon. My heart skips a beat watching the two kittens spoon. He loves his child and I love her too. But sometimes, I miss the days when it was just me and you. So, flashback to the present, I'll savor each moment. And we'll see together where Miss Universe takes us.

The End.